THE MYSTERY OF THE
Missing Pitom

Beverly Mach Geller

Dedication

For my grandson, Chaim Yosef
and his sisters and brothers: Elisheva, Shira, Nachum, Ephraim
and cousins: Baruch, Pesach, Sarah

Acknowledgements

Rabbi Shmuel Heinemann, for his knowledge about etrogim
Nachum Leib Kaplan
my husband, Sam

THE MYSTERY OF THE
Missing Pitom

Beverly Mach Geller

gefen גפן
publishing house
JERUSALEM ◆ NEW YORK

Graphic Design: Studio Paz, Jerusalem
Illustrator: Rivka-Lisa Perel

2 4 6 8 9 7 5 3 1

Gefen Publishing House
POB 36004, Jerusalem, 91360, Israel
972-2-538-0247 isragefe@netvision.net.il

Gefen Books
12 New St., Hewlett, NY 11557, USA
516-295-2805 gefenbooks@compuserve.com

www.israelbooks.com

Printed in Israel   *Send for our free catalogue*

ISBN 965-229-202-8

Library of Congress Cataloging-in-Publication Data:
Geller, Beverly Mach
The Mystery of the Missing Pitom
1. Jews - Juvenile Fiction. *[1. Jews - Fiction. 2. Sukkot - Fiction.*
3. Fasts and Feasts - Judaism - Fiction.] I. Title.

PZ7.G2786 My 1999 • [Fic]-dc21 • CIP Number : 99-052667

After Yosef, his brothers, and father finished building their *sukah*, they went to buy a *lulav* and *etrog* for the holiday of *Sukot*. Yosef's sisters, Elisheva and Shira, stayed home to help Mother.

Although Yosef was only six, he felt very grownup as he walked with *Abba*, Nachum, and Ephraim to the market.

At the market, vendors stood beside tables piled with *lulavim* and *etrogim*. Buyers crowded around the tables examining and comparing the palm branches and citrons.

After much searching, *Abba* found a perfect *lulav*. It was green, straight, not split at the top, and had lots of unopened leaves.

Then they looked for an *etrog*.

On some, the peel was too smooth. *Abba* said it had to be knobby, with more bumps.

Ephraim picked up an *etrog* but *Abba* said, "That one is too round. It should be shaped like a tower, broad at the bottom and narrower at the top."

While Yosef was looking at the huge crowd of men and boys hurrying about, Nachum found a nice *etrog*, without spots, bruises, or holes.

Abba smelled it, then held it under Yosef's nose. It smelled like honeysuckle, roses, orange blossoms – like every flower he could remember.

"Just before the holiday, I'll get the myrtle and willow branches," said *Abba*, as they left the market.

4

At home, *Abba* put the *lulav* and *etrog* on the top shelf in his study.

The next morning when Yosef woke up, he wanted more than anything else to smell the *etrog* again. But it was still three long days to *Sukot*.

Everyone was still asleep. Yosef tiptoed into the study.

High on the shelf lay the box that held the *etrog*.
He pulled over a chair and got on it. But he couldn't reach.
He found a telephone book, put it on the chair, climbed up, and
stretched out his arms.

His fingers touched the container, but he couldn't grab it.

He stood on tiptoes and stretched up - up - up. At last he lifted the container from the shelf. As he lowered his arms, the *etrog* tumbled from the box, hit the edge of the radiator, and fell to the floor.

Yosef scrambled down from the chair.

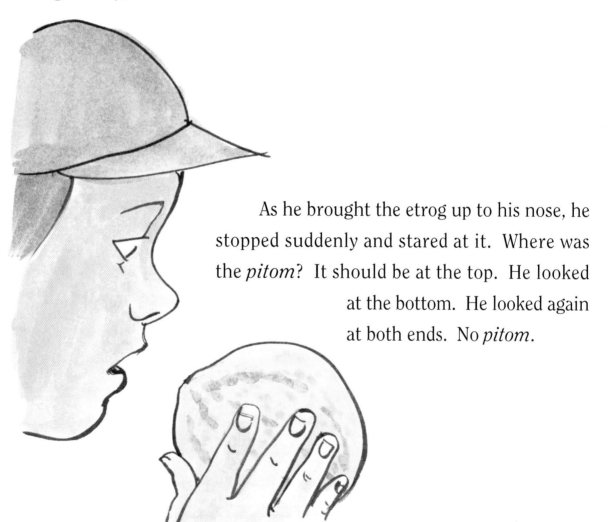

What a relief, the *etrog* looked all right. He'd put it back right away, but first he would smell it.

As he brought the etrog up to his nose, he stopped suddenly and stared at it. Where was the *pitom*? It should be at the top. He looked at the bottom. He looked again at both ends. No *pitom*.

It must have broken off when it fell. If the *pitom* came off, he knew the *etrog* could not be used for the blessing on *Sukot*.

If only he could find the *pitom*, he'd paste it back on.

He looked under the radiator. It wasn't there. Did it roll away? He looked under the chairs and desk. Not there either.

W hat should he do? Wake his parents and tell them?   No. He would wait until later.

He put the *etrog* in the box and carefully placed it back on the shelf.

During breakfast, Yosef's mouth felt like dry toast. He couldn't eat anything. Once, twice, three times he tried to tell them what had happened, but the words wouldn't come out.

He started again. "This morning..."

Someone knocked at the door and Yosef jumped up to open it.

His friends had come to play. They all ran outside.

When Yosef came home, he went to the study. He imagined that through the box he could see the *etrog* with the missing *pitom*.

He had an idea. There were *etrogim* in the store just down the street. He'd seen them when he was there with Elisheva and Shira. He would buy a different *etrog*, one with a *pitom*, and put it in the box instead.

Yosef ran to his room, pulled open the dresser drawer, and emptied his bank. He should be able to get a nice *etrog* for fourteen dollars.

He dashed to the store and bought an *etrog* with a *pitom*.

11

Finally, the first day of *Sukot* arrived.

From the shelf, *Abba* got the *lulav* that he had tied to myrtle and willow branches. Then he took down the container holding the *etrog*.

The family went into the *sukah* to make the blessing.

Abba picked up the yellowish fruit.

Would he know it's a different *etrog*?

Abba turned it right side up, then up side down. "I thought the *etrog* we bought was –uh–bigger. But maybe it shrank."

Yosef's knees felt a little weak.

"I'll put on my glasses so I can see it better," said *Abba*.

He looked again at the fruit.

Was there a smile at the corners of Abba's mouth?

"This is a fine looking *etrog*," *Abba* said, nodding his head.

"And a mysterious one, too." He paused. "More than that, this is a miraculous *etrog*. Something has happened to it that no one has ever seen before."

"What is it?" asked Shira.

"It has grown a *pitom* while waiting for *Sukot*."

Yosef's face felt hot even though a cool breeze was blowing through the *sukah*.

"We'll have to tell the Rabbi about this miracle," said *Abba*.

The words tumbled out of Yosef's mouth. "It's a different one. I wanted to smell it, but I dropped it and the *pitom* broke off. I was afraid it wouldn't be kosher for *Sukot*, so I took all my money and bought another one. I should have told you sooner. I'm sorry. I should have told you right away."

Abba patted Yosef's shoulder. "It's all right, Yosef. No harm was done."

"You didn't have to buy another one," said Nachum.

"Why not?" asked Yosef.

"This year we bought an *etrog* without a *pitom*, so there'd be no chance it might fall off accidentally." *Abba* looked at Yosef and smiled. "Little boys can get curious."

"I thought an *etrog* always has a pitom,"
said Yosef.

"Every *etrog* starts out with a *pitom* inside the flower,"
said Nachum. "But some varieties of trees lose the *pitom* very
early while the fruit is growing. They're all right to use."

"Even on regular *etrog* trees, if the *pitom* falls off while the
fruit is still growing, it's okay, too," said Ephraim.

I see that you learned your lessons well," said *Abba*. "But Yosef is also right. Usually, when the *pitom* breaks off after the *etrog* is picked, it's not kosher."

"Didn't you see there was no *pitom* when *Abba* bought it?" asked Elisheva.

Yosef shook his head.

But you learned how to choose a nice *etrog* anyway," said *Abba*.

Mother hugged Yosef and kissed his cheek. "What's important is that you told us the truth."

Yosef smiled. It was easier to tell them than he had thought.

This was going to be a happy *Sukot* after all.

Afterword

The holiday of *Sukot* is observed for eight days (seven days in Israel) in the Hebrew month of *Tishri*, which is usually during October.

On *Sukot*, Jews recall the time their ancestors lived in temporary huts in the Sinai desert. They lived there for forty years after the exodus from Egypt, before they came into the land of Israel.

Since that time, observant Jewish families build *sukahs* attached to or near their homes. During the holiday, they spend as much time as possible in the *sukah* where they have meals, entertain friends, and study *Torah*.

On each day of the holiday, either in the *sukah*, or synagogue, Jews pray while holding the four species – the *etrog, lulav*, myrtle, and willow branches. Since *Sukot* is also a harvest holiday, people praise God's abundance. The *sukah* is usually decorated with fruits and vegetables harvested in the fall.

Glossary of Hebrew Words

Abba father.

etrog citron. A fragrant citrus fruit that resembles a lemon.

lulav an unopened palm frond. It is held, together with the myrtle and willow branches, when the blessing is made.

pitom similar to a thick apple stem with a small knob (crown) at the top. Generally, if the pitom falls off after the fruit has been picked, it cannot be used for the ceremony of the blessing. Some varieties of etrogim lose the pitom at a very early growth stage and are commonly referred to as growing without a pitom. On trees that normally grow etrogim with pitomim, if the pitom falls off during the growth process, it is all right to use.

sukah temporary dwelling.

Sukot marks two events – the harvest season and the forty years Jews lived in booths in the desert before entering the land of Israel.